Nicole Robertson
Illustrated by Kimberly Groves

 LUCIDBOOKS

Unstoppable Me

Unstoppable Me is a children's book that encourages readers to love and accept themselves.

It is dedicated to all those little readers who dare to be themselves.

Unstoppable Me
Copyright © 2021 by Nicole Robertson

Published by Lucid Books in Houston, TX
www.LucidBooksPublishing.com

Illustrator: Kimberly Groves
Editor: Barbara Robertson

Paperback ISBN: 978-1-63296-444-1
Hardback ISBN: 978-1-63296-445-8
eISBN: 978-1-63296-446-5

Special Sales: Most Lucid Books titles are available in special quantity discounts.
Custom imprinting or excerpting can also be done to fit special needs.
For standard bulk orders, go to www.lucidbooksbulk.com.
For specialty press or large orders, contact Lucid Books at books@lucidbookspublishing.com.

This book belongs to _____,

and I am **UNSTOPPABLE!**

Draw yourself as a superhero!

I know a girl who wonders if she is enough.
She looks in the mirror and reflects, "Do I measure up?"

But the world sees a girl who is sweet and kind.
She is naturally thoughtful and wise.

I know a girl who wonders if she will be loved.
She looks in the mirror and daydreams, "Will I find real love?"

But the world sees a girl who is beautiful and true.
She brings joy and affection without much ado.

I know a girl who wonders if she can help others grow.
She looks in the mirror and doubts, "I don't know?"

But the world sees a girl who is patient and gentle.
She cares for all creatures that are both big and little.

I know a girl who wonders if she is unique.
She looks in the mirror and worries, "Am I complete?"

But the world sees a girl who is distinct and exceptional.
She works hard at all tasks to her highest potential.

I know a girl who wonders if she will succeed.
She looks in the mirror and questions, "Could it be me?"

But the world sees a girl who is intelligent and brave.
She is smart and fearless in so many ways.

I know a girl who wonders if she can make a difference.
She looks in the mirror and considers, "Am I significant?"

But the world sees a girl who celebrates diversity.
She conducts selfless acts with the utmost sincerity.

You, little girl,
are everything and more.

An unstoppable force!
You are hard-core!

Look in the mirror and wonder no more.
Believe in yourself and say it once more:

"I am ENOUGH! I will SUCCEED!"
"I can be anything I want to be."

"I am LOVED! I will help others GROW!"
"I am colorful like a rainbow."

"I am UNIQUE! I will make a DIFFERENCE!"
"I am marvelous and significant."

"I know a girl."

Love is one of our superpowers!

Did you notice that there are hearts hidden throughout the book?

Challenge:
Can you find a heart on each page?

Super Challenge:
Can you find all 80 hearts hidden throughout the pages of this book?

Hint: There are 8 on this page!

A huge thank you to my 111 Kickstarter backers!
The success of *Unstoppable Me* would not have
been possible without each one of YOU!

Nicole Robertson strives to create compelling children's books with fun, educational, and purposeful messages that empower and encourage self-esteem in readers of any age. She is a wife and also a mother of two happy children who love to laugh, use their imaginations, and read books. Nicole aspires to promote language development in readers by helping them imitate sounds, recognize patterns, and learn new words to EMPOWER them!

CPSIA information can be obtained
at www.ICGtesting.com
Printed in the USA
BVHW021358270421
605946BV00008B/1305